Black Beauty

Black Beauty

Abridged from the original by
Anna Sewell

Illustrations by
Francesca Greco

CD narrated by
Jonathan Keeble

SOURCEBOOKS
Jabberwocky
AN IMPRINT OF SOURCEBOOKS

© 2008 by Naxos AudioBooks Ltd.
Cover and internal design © 2008 by Sourcebooks, Inc.
Internal illustrations by Francesca Greco
Cover illustration by C. Shana Greger

Sourcebooks and the colophon are registered trademarks of Sourcebooks, Inc.

Published by Sourcebooks Jabberwocky, an imprint of Sourcebooks, Inc.
P.O. Box 4410, Naperville, Illinois 60567-4410
(630) 961-3900
Fax: (630) 961-2168
www.sourcebooks.com

Library of Congress Cataloging-in-Publication Data

Sewell, Anna.
    Black Beauty : the autobiography of a horse / Anna Sewell.
       p. cm.
    ISBN-13: 978-1-4022-1168-3 (hardcover : alk. paper)
    ISBN-10: 1-4022-1168-6 (hardcover : alk. paper) 1. Horses—Juvenile fiction. [1. Horses—Fiction. 2. Great Britain--History--19th century--Fiction.] I. Title. Accompanying CD has narration, music, and sound effects.

PZ10.3.S38Bl 2008
[Fic]--dc22

                                    2007044114

                Printed and bound in the United States of America.
                    LBM 10 9 8 7 6 5 4 3 2 1

CONTENTS

Chapter 1

THE HUNT

The first place that I can well remember was a large pleasant meadow with a pond of clear water. Some shady trees leaned over it, rushes and water-lilies grew at the deep end. Over the hedge on one side we looked into a ploughed field, and on the other we looked over a gate at our master's house, which stood by the roadside.

While I was young I lived upon my mother's milk, as I could not eat grass. In the daytime I ran by her side, and at night I lay down close by her. When it was hot we used to stand by the pond in the shade of the trees, and when it was cold we had a nice warm shed near a grove.

One day my mother said to me, "I hope you will grow up gentle and good, and never learn bad ways; do your work with a good will, lift your feet up well when you trot, and never bite or kick even in play."

Before I was two years old a circumstance happened which I have never forgotten. It was early in the spring; there had been a little frost in the night, and a light mist hung over the woods and meadows. I and the other colts were feeding at the lower part of the field when we heard, quite in the distance, what sounded like the cry of dogs. The oldest of the colts pricked his ears, and said, "There are the hounds!" and cantered off, followed by the rest of us, to the upper part of the field, where we could look over the hedge. My mother and an old riding horse of our master's were also standing near.

"They have found a hare," said my mother, "and if they come this way we shall see the hunt."

And soon the dogs were all tearing down the field of young wheat next to ours. I never heard such a noise. They did not bark, but kept up a "yo! yo, o, o! yo! yo, o, o!" at the top of their voices. After them came a number of men on horseback, some of them in green coats, all galloping as fast as they could.

"Now we shall see the hare," said my mother; and just then a hare

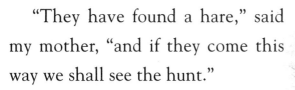

wild with fright rushed by and made for the woods. On came the dogs; they burst over the bank, leaped the stream, and came dashing across the field followed by the huntsmen.

Six or eight men leaped their horses clean over, close upon the dogs. The hare tried to get through the fence; it was too thick, and she turned sharp round to make for the road, but it was too late; the dogs were upon her with their wild cries; and that was the end of her.

I was so astonished that I did not at first see what was going on by the brook; but when I did look there was a sad sight; two fine horses were down, one was struggling in the stream, and the other was groaning on the grass. One of the riders was getting out of the water covered with mud, the other lay quite still.

"His neck is broken," said my mother.

"And serve him right, too," said one of the colts.

"Well, no," she said, "you must not say that; but I never yet could make out why men are so fond of this sport; they often hurt themselves, often spoil good horses, and tear up the fields, and all for a hare or a fox, or a stag; but we are only horses, and don't know."

Many of the riders had gone to the young man; but my master, who had been watching what was going on, was the first to raise him. His head fell back and his arms hung down, and everyone looked very serious. There was no noise now; even the dogs were quiet. They carried him to our master's house. I heard afterward that it was young George Gordon, the squire's only son, a fine, tall young man, and the pride of his family.

When Mr. Bond, the farrier, came to look at the black horse groaning on the grass, he shook his head; one of his legs was broken. Then some one ran to our master's house and came back with a gun; presently there was a loud bang, and then all was still; the black horse moved no more.

A farrier is someone who specializes in the care of horses' hoofs. Farriers also work as blacksmiths and forge the metal shoes horses wear.

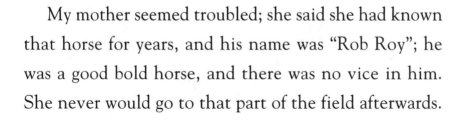

My mother seemed troubled; she said she had known that horse for years, and his name was "Rob Roy"; he was a good bold horse, and there was no vice in him. She never would go to that part of the field afterwards.

Chapter 2

MY BREAKING IN

I was now beginning to grow handsome; my coat had grown fine and soft, and was bright black. I had one white foot and a pretty white star on my forehead. I was thought very handsome.

When I was four years old Squire Gordon came to look at me. He examined my eyes, my mouth, and my legs; he felt them all down; and then I had to walk and trot and gallop before him. He said,

"When he has been well broken in he will do very well."

My master said he would break me in himself, as he should not like me to be frightened or hurt, and he lost no time about it, for the next day he began.

Breaking means to teach a horse to wear a saddle and bridle, and to carry on his back a man, woman or child. Besides this he has to learn to wear a collar, a crupper, and a breeching, and to stand still while they are put on; then to have a cart or a chaise fixed behind. He must never start at what he sees, nor speak to other horses, nor bite, nor kick, nor have any will of his own; but always do his master's, even though he may be very tired or hungry. But worst of all, when his harness is once on, he may neither jump for joy nor lie down for weariness.

Those who have never had a bit in their mouths cannot think how bad it feels; a great piece of cold hard steel as thick as a man's finger to be pushed into one's mouth, between one's teeth, and over one's tongue, with the ends coming out at the corner of your mouth, and held fast there by straps over your head, under your throat, round your nose, and under your chin; it is very bad! Yes, very bad! At least I thought so.

The saddle, was not half so bad; my master put it on my back very gently. I had a few oats, then a little leading about. This he did every day till I began to look for the oats and the saddle. One morning, my master got on my back and rode me round the meadow on the soft grass. It certainly did feel queer; but I must say I felt rather proud to carry my master, and as he continued

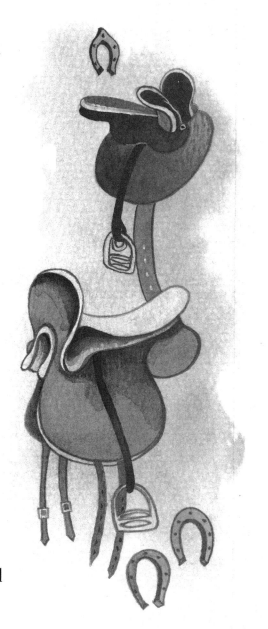

to ride me a little every day I soon became accustomed to it.

The next unpleasant business was putting on the iron shoes. My master went with me to the smith's forge, to see that I was not hurt or got any fright. The blacksmith took my feet in his hand, one after the other, and cut away some of the hoof. It did not pain me, so I stood still on three legs till he had done them all. Then he took a piece of iron the shape of my foot, and clapped it on, and drove some nails through the shoe quite into my hoof, so that the shoe was firmly on. My feet felt very stiff and heavy, but in time I got used to it.

My master went on to break me to harness. There were new things to wear. First, a stiff heavy collar just on my neck, and a bridle with great side-pieces against my eyes called blinkers, and blinkers they were, for I could not see on either side, but only straight in front of me; next, there was a small saddle with a nasty stiff strap that went right under my tail; that was the crupper. I hated the crupper. I never felt more like kicking, but in time I got used to everything.

Chapter 3

A Fair Start

Early one May, there came a man from Squire Gordon's, who took me to the Hall. My master said, "Goodbye, Darkie; be a good horse." I could not say goodbye, I put my nose into his hand; he patted me kindly, and I left my first home.

Squire Gordon's park skirted the village of Birtwick. It was entered by a large iron gate, at which stood the first lodge. Then you trotted along on a smooth road between clumps of large old trees; then another lodge and another gate, which brought you to the house and the gardens. Beyond this lay the home paddock, the old orchard, and the stables. There was accommodation for

many horses. The stable into which I was taken was very roomy, with four good stalls. A large swinging window opened into the yard made it pleasant and airy.

The first stall was a large square one, shut in behind with a wooden gate; the others were not nearly so, it was called a loose box, because the horse that was put into it was not tied up, but left to do as he liked. It is a great thing to

have a loose box. Into this fine box the groom put me. He gave me some very nice oats, he patted me, spoke kindly, and then went away.

In the stall next to mine stood a little fat grey pony, with a thick mane and tail, a very pretty head, and a pert little nose.

I said, "How do you do? What is your name?"

He turned round as far as his halter would allow, held up his head, and said,

"My name is Merrylegs. I carry the young ladies on my back, and sometimes I take our mistress out in the low chair. They think a great deal of me, and so does James. Are you going to live next door to me? I hope you are good-tempered; I do not like anyone next door who bites."

The difference between a horse and a pony is that a pony is less than 14.2 hands high, while a horse is more than 14.2 hands high. Horses and ponies are measured in units called "hands." "Hands high" literally refers to how many human hands it takes to measure the size of the horse from the ground to the ridge between its shoulder blades. One hand is approximately four inches long, so a pony or horse that is 14.2 hands high is about 57 inches tall.

Just then a horse's head looked over from the stall beyond; the ears were laid back, and the eye looked rather ill-tempered. This was a tall chestnut mare, with a long handsome neck. She looked across and said:

"So it is you who have turned me out of my box; it is a very strange thing for a colt like you to come and turn a lady out of her own home."

"I beg your pardon," I said, "I have turned no one out; the man who brought me put me here. I had nothing to do with it; and as to my being a colt, I am turned four years old and a grown-up horse. I never had words yet with horse or mare, and it is my wish to live at peace."

"Well," she said, "we shall see."

In the afternoon, when she went out, Merrylegs told me all about it.

"The thing is," said Merrylegs, "Ginger has a bad habit of biting and snapping; that is why they call her Ginger. In the loose box she used to snap very much. One day she bit James in the arm and made it bleed, and so Miss Flora and Miss Jessie, who are very fond of me, were afraid to come into the stable. They used to bring me nice things to eat. I hope they will come again, if you do not bite or snap."

I told him I never bit anything, and could not think what pleasure Ginger found in it.

"Well, I don't think she does find pleasure," says Merrylegs; "it is just a bad habit; she says no one was ever kind to her, why should she not bite? I think she might be good-tempered here. You see," he said, with a wise look, "I know a great deal, and I can tell you there is not a better place for a horse all round the country than this. John is the best groom that ever was; he has been here fourteen years; and you never saw such a kind boy as James; so that it is all Ginger's own fault that she did not stay in that box."

The name of the coachman was John Manly; he had a wife and one little child, and they lived in the coachman's cottage, very near the stables. The next day after breakfast he came and fitted me with a bridle. He rode me first slowly, then at a trot, then a canter, and when we were on the common he gave me a light touch with his whip, and we had a splendid gallop. As we came back through the park, we met the squire and Mrs. Gordon walking; John jumped off.

"Well, John, how does he go?"

"First-rate, sir," answered John; "he is as fleet as a deer, a fine spirit too; but the lightest touch of the rein will guide him. They were shooting rabbits near the Highwood, and a gun went off close by; he pulled up a little and looked, but did not stir a step to right or left. I just held the rein steady and did not hurry him, and it's my opinion he has not been frightened or ill-used while he was young."

"I will try him myself to-morrow," said the squire.

The next day I was brought up for my master. I tried to do exactly what he wanted me to do. He was a very good rider, and thoughtful for his horse too. When he came home the lady was at the hall door as he rode up.

"Well, my dear," she said, "how do you like him?"

"Oh, he is exactly what John said," he replied; "a pleasanter creature I never wish to mount. What shall we call him?"

"Would you like Ebony?" she said; "he is as black as ebony."

"No, not Ebony."

"Will you call him Blackbird, that's your uncle's old horse?"

"No, he is far handsomer than old Blackbird ever was."

"He is really quite a beauty, and he has such a sweet, good-tempered face, and such a fine, intelligent eye—what do you say to calling him Black Beauty?"

"Black Beauty—why, yes, I think that is a very good name."

When John went into the stable he told James that master and mistress had chosen a good, sensible English name for me. They both laughed. James said, "Well, if it was not for bringing back the past, I should have named him Rob Roy, for I never saw two horses more alike."

"That's no wonder," said John; "didn't you know that Farmer Grey's old Duchess was the mother of them both?"

I had never heard that before. Poor Rob Roy who was killed at that hunt was my brother! I did not wonder that my mother was so troubled.

John seemed very proud of me; he used to make my mane and tail smooth as a lady's hair, and he would talk to me a great deal. I grew very fond of him, he was so gentle and kind. James Howard, the stable boy, was just as gentle and pleasant in his way, I thought myself well-off.

A few days after this I had to go out with Ginger in the carriage. I wondered how we should get on together; but except laying her ears back when I was led up to her, she behaved very well. She did her full share, and I never wish to have a better partner in double harness. As for Merrylegs, he and I soon became great friends.

Chapter 4

LIFE AT BIRTWICK

$\mathcal{I}$ was quite happy in my new place, and if there was one thing that I missed it must not be thought I was discontented. For three years and a half of my life I had had all the liberty I could wish for; but now, week after week, month after month, and no doubt year after year, I must stand up in a stable night and day except when I am wanted, and then I must be just as steady and quiet as any old horse who has worked twenty years. Straps here and straps there, a bit in my mouth, and blinkers over my eyes.

I ought to say that sometimes we had our liberty for a few hours in the home paddock or the old orchard;

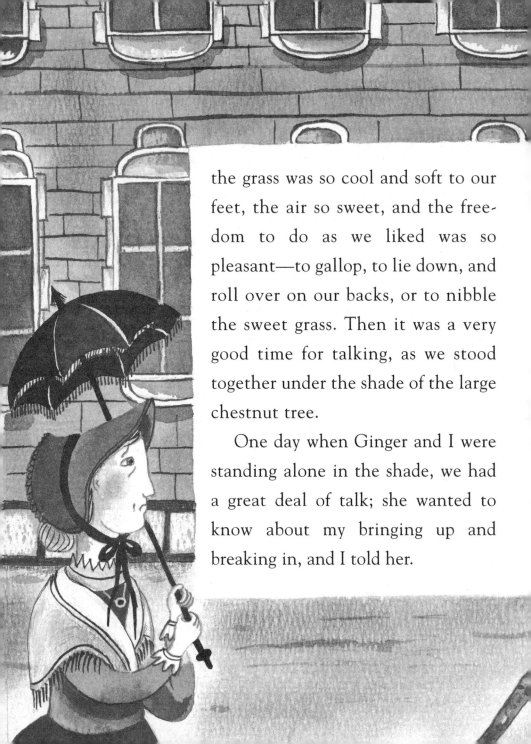

the grass was so cool and soft to our feet, the air so sweet, and the freedom to do as we liked was so pleasant—to gallop, to lie down, and roll over on our backs, or to nibble the sweet grass. Then it was a very good time for talking, as we stood together under the shade of the large chestnut tree.

One day when Ginger and I were standing alone in the shade, we had a great deal of talk; she wanted to know about my bringing up and breaking in, and I told her.

"Well," said she, "if I had had your bringing up I might have had as good a temper as you, but now I don't believe I ever shall. I never had any-one, horse or man, that was kind to me, or that I cared to please. I was taken from my mother as soon as I was weaned, there was no kind master like yours to look after me. When it came to breaking in, oh that was a bad time. By then I had made up my mind that men were my natural enemies. I bit James once pretty sharp, but John said, "Try her with kindness," and instead of punishing me as I expected, James brought me a bran mash and stroked me and I have never snapped at him since, and I won't either."

I was sorry for Ginger, but as the weeks went on she grew much more gentle and cheerful, and one day James said, "I do believe that mare is getting fond of me, she quite whinnied after me."

"Ay, ay, Jim," said John, "she'll be as good as Black Beauty by and by."

The longer I lived at Birtwick the more proud and happy I felt at having such a place. Our master and mistress were respected and beloved by all who knew them; good and kind to everybody and everything.

If mistress met a heavily laden horse with his head strained up she would stop the carriage and get out, and reason with the driver in her sweet serious voice, and try to show him how foolish and cruel it was. I don't think any man could withstand our mistress. I wish all ladies were like her.

Bearing reins were used in the 19th century to elevate carriage horses' heads and necks into an arched shape. This was done mostly for appearance and it was often painful for the horses. Bearing reins were eventually banned with the help of the book *Black Beauty*.

Chapter 5

THE STORM AND THE FIRE

One day late in the autumn my master had a long journey to go on business. John went with his master and I was put into the dog-cart. There had been a great deal of rain, and now the wind was very high. We went along merrily till we came to the toll-gate and the low wooden bridge. The man there said the river was rising fast, and he feared it would be a bad night. Many of the meadows were under water. In one low part of the road the water was halfway up to my knees.

When we got to town the master's business engaged him a long time. We did not start for home till rather late in the afternoon. I heard the master say

to John that he had never been out in such a storm. By the time we got back to the bridge it was nearly dark. The water was over the middle of it; that happened sometimes when the floods were out, but the moment my feet touched the first part of the bridge I

felt sure there was something wrong.
I made a dead stop.

"Go on, Beauty," said my master,
and he gave me a touch with the
whip, but I dare not stir; he gave me
a sharp cut; I jumped, but I dare not
go forward.

"Come on, Beauty, what's the
matter?"

John sprang out of the dog-cart
and came to my head. He looked all
about. I could not tell him, but I
knew the bridge was not safe.

Just then the man at the toll-gate on the other side ran out.

"Hoy, hoy, hoy! Halloo! Stop!" he cried. "The bridge is broken in the middle, and part of it is carried away; if you come on you'll be into the river."

"Thank God!" said my master. "You Beauty!" said John, and turned me round to the road by the river-side.

At last we saw a light at the hall door and as we came up, mistress ran out and said, "Are you really safe, my dear? Oh! I have been so anxious, fancying all sorts of things."

"If your Black Beauty had not been wiser than we were we should all have been carried down the river at the wooden bridge."

I heard no more, as they went into the house, and John took me to the stable. Oh, what a good supper he gave me that night, a good bran mash and some crushed beans with my oats, and such a thick bed of straw! I was glad of it, for I was tired.

One day it was decided by my master and mistress to pay a visit to some friends who lived about forty-six miles from our home. James was to drive. The first day we travelled thirty-two miles. There were some long, heavy hills, but James drove so carefully and thoughtfully that we were not at all harassed. As the sun was going down we reached the town where we were to spend the night.

We stopped at the principal hotel, and two hostlers came to take us out. The head hostler was a pleasant, active little man, with a crooked leg, and a yellow striped waistcoat. I never saw a man unbuckle harness so quickly as he did, and with a pat and a good word he led me to a long stable, with two or three horses in it.

Later on in the evening a traveller's horse was brought in and while he was cleaning him a young man with a pipe in his mouth lounged into the stable to gossip.

"I say, Towler," said the hostler, "just run up the ladder into the loft and put some hay down into this horse's rack, will you? Only lay down your pipe."

"All right," said the other, and went up through the trapdoor; and I heard him step across the floor overhead and put down the hay. James came in to look at us the last thing, and then the door was locked.

I cannot say how long I had slept, but I woke up very uncomfortable. The stable seemed full of smoke, and I hardly knew how to breathe. I listened, and heard a soft rushing sort of noise and a low crackling and snapping. I did not know what it was, but there was something in the sound so strange that it made me tremble all over. The other horses were all awake; some were pulling at their halters, stamping.

At last I heard steps outside, and the young hostler burst into the stable with a lantern and began to untie the horses, and try to lead them out; but he seemed in such a hurry and so frightened himself that he frightened me still more. The first horse would not go with him; he tried the second and third, and they too would not stir. He tried us all by turns and then left the stable.

No doubt we were very foolish, but danger seemed to be all round, and there was nobody we knew to trust in, and all was strange and uncertain. I looked upward and saw a red light flickering on the wall. Then I heard a cry of "Fire!" and the old hostler came in; quietly and quickly he got one horse out, and went to another, the roaring overhead was dreadful.

The next thing I heard was James' voice, quiet and cheery, as it always was.

"Come on, my beauties, time for us to be off, wake up and come along." He came to me first, patting me as he came in.

"Come, Beauty, on with your bridle, that's my boy, we'll soon be out of this smother." He took the scarf off his neck, and tied it lightly over my eyes, and patting and coaxing led me out of the stable. Safe in the yard, he slipped the scarf off my eyes, and shouted, "Here somebody! Take this horse while I go back for the other."

Sometimes horses are blindfolded to lead them into
and out of trailers or other places they will not go.

A man stepped forward and took me, and James darted
back into the stable. I set up a shrill whinny as I saw him
go. Ginger told me afterward that whinny was the best
thing I could have done for her, for had she not heard me
outside she would never have had courage to come out.

Presently I heard above all the stir and din a loud,
clear voice, which I knew was my master's:

"James Howard! James Howard! Are you there?"

There was no answer, but I heard a crash of something falling in the stable, and the next moment I gave
a loud, joyful neigh, for I saw James coming through the
smoke leading Ginger with him; she was coughing
violently, and he was not able to speak.

"My brave lad!" said master, laying his hand on his shoulder, "are you hurt?" James shook his head, for he could not yet speak.

"Ay," said the man who held me; "he is a brave lad, and no mistake."

"Now," said master, "when you have got your breath, James, we'll get out of this place as quickly as we can," and we were moving toward the entry, when from the marketplace there came a sound of galloping feet and loud rumbling wheels.

"'Tis the fire-engine! The fire-engine!" shouted two or three voices, "Stand back, make way!" and clattering and thundering over the stones two horses dashed into the yard with a heavy engine behind them. The firemen leaped to the ground; there was no need to ask where the fire was—it was rolling up in a great blaze from the roof.

We got out as fast as we could into the broad quiet marketplace; the stars were shining, and except the

noise behind us, all was still. Master
led the way to a large hotel on the
other side, and as soon as the hostler
came, he said, "James, I must now
hasten to your mistress; I trust the
horses entirely to you, order what-
ever you think is needed," and with
that he was gone.

There was a dreadful sound before
we got into our stalls—the shrieks of

those poor horses that were left burning to death in the stable—very terrible! And made both Ginger and me feel very bad. We, however, were taken in and well done by.

Chapter 6

GOING FOR THE DOCTOR

The rest of the journey was very easy, and a little after sunset we reached the house of my master's friend. We stopped two or three days at this place and then returned home. All went well on the journey, John was glad to see us. Before he and James left us for the night James said,

"Who is coming in my place?"

"Little Joe Green at the lodge," said John.

"Little Joe Green? Why, he's a child!"

"He is fourteen and a half," said John. "He is quick and willing, and kind-hearted, too, and wishes very much to come. I said I was quite agreeable to try him for six weeks."

"Six weeks!" said James; "It will be six months before he can be of much use! It will make you a deal of work, John."

"Well," said John with a laugh, "work and I are very good friends; I never was afraid of work yet."

"You are a very good man," said James. "I wish I may ever be like you."

Joe came to the stables to learn all he could before James left. He was a nice little bright fellow, and always came whistling to his work.

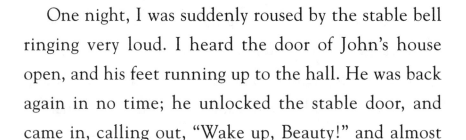

One night, I was suddenly roused by the stable bell ringing very loud. I heard the door of John's house open, and his feet running up to the hall. He was back again in no time; he unlocked the stable door, and came in, calling out, "Wake up, Beauty!" and almost before I could think, he had got the saddle on my back and the bridle on my head and took me at a quick trot up to the hall door. The squire stood there, with a lamp in his hand.

"Now, John," he said, "ride for your life—that is, for your mistress's life; there is not a moment to lose. Give this note to Dr. White; give your horse a rest at the inn, and be back as soon as you can."

John said, "Yes, sir," and he was on my back in a minute. "Now, Beauty, do your best."

I galloped as fast as I could lay my feet on the ground; I don't believe that my old grandfather, who won the race at Newmarket, could have gone faster. After eight miles run we came to the town. The church clock struck three as we drew up at Dr. White's door. John rang the bell, and knocked at the door like thunder. A window was thrown up, and Dr. White, in his night cap, put his head out and said, "What do you want?"

"Mrs. Gordon is very ill, sir; master wants you to go at once; he thinks she will die if you cannot get there."

"Wait," he said. He shut the window, and was soon at the door.

"The worst of it is," he said, "that my horse has been out all day and is quite done up;

my son has just been sent for, and he has taken the other. Can I have your horse?"

"He has come at a gallop nearly all the way, sir, and I was to give him a rest here; but I think my master would not be against it, if you think fit, sir."

"All right," he said; "I will soon be ready."

I will not tell about our way back. The doctor was a heavier man than John, and not so good a rider; however, I did my very best. When we came to the hill the doctor drew me up.

"Now, my good fellow," he said, "take some breath."

I was glad he did, for I was nearly spent, but that breathing helped me on, and soon we were in the park. The doctor went into the house and Joe led me to the stable. I was glad to get home; my legs shook under me, and I could only stand and pant. I had not a dry hair on my body, and I steamed all over. Poor Joe! As yet he knew very little, but I am sure he did the best he knew. He rubbed my legs and my chest, but he did not put my warm cloth on me; he thought I was so hot I should not like it. Then he gave me a pailful of water; it was very cold and very good, and I drank it all; then he gave me some hay and some corn, and thinking he had done right, he went away.

I was very ill; a strong inflammation had attacked my lungs, and John nursed me night and day. My master, too, often came to see me.

"My poor Beauty," he said one day, "my good horse, you saved your mistress's life, Beauty; yes, you saved her life."

One night John had to give me a draught; Thomas Green, Joe's father came in to help him. After I had taken it and John had made me as comfortable as he could, he said he should stay half an hour to see how the medicine settled. Joe's father said he would stay with him.

For a while both men sat silent, and then Tom Green said in a low voice:

"I wish, John, that you'd say a kind word to Joe. The boy is quite broken-hearted. He says he knows it was all his fault, though he is sure he did the best he knew, and he says if Beauty dies no-one will ever speak to him again. It goes to my heart. Just a word; he is not a bad boy."

After a short pause John said slowly, "I know he meant no harm, I never said he did; I know he is not a bad boy. But you see, that horse is

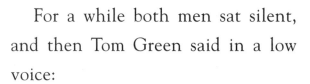

the pride of my heart; and to think that his life may be flung away in this manner is more than I can bear. But I will try to-morrow."

"John, thank you. I knew you did not wish to be too hard, and I am glad that you see it was only ignorance."

John's voice almost startled me as he answered: "Only ignorance! Only ignorance! Don't you know that it is the worst thing in the world, next to wickedness? If people can say, 'Oh! I did not know, I did not mean any harm,' they think it is all right. You were a good deal cut up yourself, Tom, two weeks ago, when those young ladies left your hothouse door open, with a frosty east wind blowing right in. You said it killed a good many of your plants. And yet," said John, "I am sure they did not mean it; it was only ignorance."

I heard no more of this conversation, for the medicine did well and sent me to sleep, and in the morning I felt much better; but I often thought of John's words when I came to know more of the world.

Chapter 7

THE ACCIDENT WITH REUBEN SMITH

Now I had lived in this happy place three years, but sad changes were about to come over us. Our mistress was ill, and the doctor was often at the house. Then we heard that she must leave her home at once, and go to a warm country for two or three years. The news fell upon the household like the tolling of a deathbell.

John went about his work silent and sad, and Joe scarcely whistled. Master sold Ginger and me to his old friend, the Earl, for he thought we should have a good place there. Merrylegs he had given to the vicar, who was wanting a pony for Mrs. Blomefield, but it was on the condition that he should never be sold. Joe was engaged to take care of him, so I thought that Merrylegs was well off. John had the offer of several good places, but he said he should wait a little and look around.

The evening before they left, the master came to the stable to give his horses the last pat. He seemed very low-spirited; I knew that by his voice. The master thanked him for his long and faithful service; but that was too much for John.

"Pray, don't, sir, I can't bear it; you and my dear mistress have done so much for me that I could never repay it. We shall never forget you, sir, and please God, we may some day see mistress back again like herself; we must keep up hope, sir." Master gave John his hand and they both left the stable.

The last sad day had come. Ginger and I brought the carriage up to the hall door for the last time. The master came down the steps carrying the mistress in his arms.

He placed her carefully in the carriage, while the house servants stood round crying.

"Good-by, again," he said; "we shall not forget any of you," and he got in.

The next morning John put the saddle on Ginger and the leading rein on me, and rode us across the country to Earlshall Park, where the Earl lived. We went into the yard through a stone gateway, and John asked for Mr. York. It was some time before he came. He was a fine-looking, middle-aged man, and his voice said at once that he expected to be obeyed. He was very friendly and polite to John, and called a groom to take us to our boxes. We were taken to a light, airy stable, adjoining each other, where we were rubbed down and fed. In about half an hour John and Mr. York, who was to be our new coachman, came in to see us.

"Now, Mr. Manly," he said, after carefully looking at us both, "I can see no fault in these horses; but we all know that horses have their peculiarities as well as men. I should like to know if there is anything particular in either of these that you would like to mention."

"Well," said John, "The black one has never known a hard word or a blow since he was foaled, and all his pleasure seems to be to do what you wish; but the chestnut must have had some bad treatment. She came to us snappish, but when she found what sort of place ours was, it all went off by degrees. If she is well treated there is not a better, more willing animal than she is."

"Of course," said York, "I quite understand; but you know it is not easy in stables like these to have all the grooms just what they should be. I'll do my best and remember what you have said about the mare."

Early in the spring, the Earl and part of his family went up to London, and took York with them. I and Ginger and some other horses were left at home, and the head groom was left in charge.

No one more thoroughly understood his business than Reuben Smith, but he had one great fault; the love of drink.

It was now early in April, and the family was expected home some time in May. The light brougham was to be fresh done up, and it was arranged that Smith should drive to the town in it, and ride back; for this purpose he took the saddle with him. I was chosen for the journey. We left the carriage at the maker's, and Smith rode me to the White Lion, and ordered the hostler to feed me, and have me ready for him at four o'clock.

A brougham is a type of carriage that has four wheels and an enclosed seating area for the passengers. The driver sits outside of the passenger compartment in the open air.

A nail in one of my front shoes had started as I came along, but the hostler did not notice it till just about four o'clock. Smith did not come into the yard till five, and then he said he should not leave till six, as he had met with some old friends. The man then told him of the nail, and asked if he should have the shoe looked to.

"No," said Smith, "all right till we get home."

He spoke in a very loud, offhand way. I thought it unlike him not to see about loose nails in our shoes. It was nearly nine o'clock before he called for me, in a loud, rough voice. He seemed to be in a very bad temper. The land-lord stood at the door and said,

"Have a care, Mr. Smith!"

But he answered with an oath; and almost before he

was out of the town he began to gallop, frequently giving me a sharp cut with his whip. The roads were stony, going over them at this pace, my shoe became looser, and as we neared the turnpike gate it came off but Smith was too drunk to notice.

Beyond the turnpike was a long piece of road, upon which fresh stones had just been laid—large sharp stones. Over this road I was forced to gallop and my shoeless foot suffered dreadfully; the hoof was broken and split and the inside was terribly cut by the sharpness of the stones. I stumbled, and fell on my knees. Smith was flung off with great force.

I recovered my feet and limped to the side of the road. The moon had just risen above the hedge, and by its light I could see Smith lying a few yards beyond me. He did not rise. I could do nothing for him nor myself, but, oh, how I listened for the sound of horse, or wheels, or footsteps! It was a calm, sweet April night; there were no sounds but a few low notes of a nightingale.

It must have been nearly midnight when I heard horses' feet. I neighed loudly, and was overjoyed to hear an answering neigh from Ginger, and men's voices. They came slowly over the

stones, and stopped at the dark figure that lay upon the ground.

One of the men jumped out, and stooped down over it.

"It is Reuben. He's dead," he said; "feel how cold his hands are."

They came and looked at me. They soon saw my cut knees.

"Why, the horse has been down and thrown him! Who would have thought the black horse would have done that? Odd, too, that the horse has not moved from the place."

Robert, the groom, then attempted to lead me. I made a step, but almost fell again.

"Look here—his hoof is cut all to pieces; he might well come down! I tell you what, Ned, I'm afraid it hasn't been all right with Reuben. Just think of his riding a horse over these stones without a shoe! I'm afraid it has been the old thing over again."

Robert took his handkerchief and bound it closely round my

hoof, and led me home. I shall never forget that night walk. Robert led me very slowly and I limped and hobbled as well as I could.

The next day the farrier examined my wounds. He said he hoped the joint was not injured but I should never lose the blemish.

Chapter 8

A RUINED HORSE

As soon as my knees were sufficiently healed I was turned into a small meadow for a month or two. No other creature was there; and though I enjoyed the liberty and the sweet grass, I felt lonely. I often neighed when I heard horses' feet passing in the road, but I seldom got an answer; till one morning the gate opened, and who should come in but dear old Ginger.

With a joyful whinny I trotted up to her, but I soon found that it was not for our pleasure that she was brought to be with me. She had been ruined by Lord George, a hard rider, quite careless of his horse. Her wind was touched. Besides which he was too heavy for her, and her back was strained.

"So," she said, "here we are, ruined in our prime, you by a drunkard, I by a fool; it is very hard."

One day we saw the Earl come into the meadow, and York was with him. The Earl seemed much annoyed.

"Three hundred pounds flung away for no earthly use," said he; "These horses of my old friend, who thought they would find a good home with me, are ruined. The black one must be sold, I could not have knees like these in my stables."

About a week after this I was bought by the master of the livery stables in Bath. These stables were not so airy and pleasant as those I had been used to. The stalls were laid on a slope instead of being level, and as my head was kept tied to the manger, I was obliged always to stand on the slope, which was very fatiguing. However, I was well fed and well cleaned, and our master took as much care of us as he could.

Hitherto I had always been driven by people who at least knew how to drive; but in this place I was to get my experience of the different kinds of bad driving. I was a "job horse," let out to all sorts of people who wished to hire me. As I was good-tempered and gentle, I was let out to the ignorant drivers because I could be depended upon.

There were the tight-rein drivers—men who seemed to think that all depended on holding the reins as hard as they could, never relaxing the pull on the horse's mouth. Then there are the loose-rein drivers, who let the reins lie easily on our backs, and their own hands rest lazily on their knees. Such gentlemen have no control over a horse, if anything happens suddenly. Then there is the steam-engine style of driving; these drivers seemed to think that a horse was something like a steam-engine, only smaller. They think that a horse is bound to go just as far and just as fast and with just as heavy a load as they please. This driving wears us out faster than any other kind.

Anna Sewell wrote Black Beauty to promote fair treatment of animals, especially horses. It is considered one of the most influential animal rights books ever written.

Of course we sometimes came in for good driving. One morning I was put into the light gig, and taken to a house in Pulteney Street. Two gentlemen came out; the taller of them came round to my head; he looked at the bit and bridle, and just shifted the collar with his hand, to see if it fitted comfortably.

"Do you consider this horse wants a curb?" he said to the hostler. "Well," said the man, "I should say he would go just as well without; he has an uncommon good mouth."

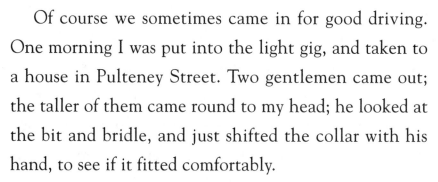

"I don't like it," said the gentleman; "be so good as to take it off, and put the rein in at the cheek. An easy mouth is a great thing on a long journey, is it not, old fellow?" he said, patting my neck.

Then he took the reins, and they both got up. I arched my neck and set off at my best pace. I had someone behind me who knew how a good horse ought to be driven. It seemed like old times again, and made me feel quite gay.

This gentleman took a great liking to me, and after trying me several times with the saddle, he prevailed upon my master to sell me to a friend of his, who wanted a safe, pleasant horse for riding. And so it came to pass that in the summer I was sold to Mr. Barry.

My new master lived at Bath, and was much engaged in business. He hired a stable a short distance from his lodgings, and engaged a man named Filcher as groom. My master knew very little about horses, but he treated me well, and I should have had a good and easy place but for circumstances of which he was ignorant. My groom understood his business. He had been a hostler in one of the great hotels in Bath.

Grooms and hostlers both take care of horses in stables. However, a hostler usually works at an inn or hotel.

After a while it seemed to me that my oats came very short. In two or three weeks this began to tell upon my strength and spirits. I wondered that my master did not see that something was the matter. If I could have spoken I could have told my master where his oats went. My groom used to come every morning about six o'clock with a little boy. He used to go with his father into the harness-room, where the corn was kept, and I could see them, when the door stood ajar, fill a little bag with oats out of the bin, and then he used to be off.

Five or six mornings after this, the door was pushed open, and a policeman walked in, holding the child tight by the arm; another policeman followed. Filcher was cleaning my feet at the time, but they soon saw him, and though he blustered a good deal they walked him off to the "lock-up" and his boy with him. I heard afterwards that the boy was not held to be guilty, but the man was sentenced to prison.

In a few days my new groom came. He was a tall, good-looking fellow; but if ever there was a humbug in the shape of a groom, Alfred Smirk was the man. He always brushed my mane and tail with water and my hoofs with oil before he brought me to the door, to make me look smart; but as to cleaning my feet or looking to my shoes, or grooming me thoroughly, he thought no more of that than if I had been a cow.

He never took all the straw away, and the smell from what lay underneath was very bad. But that was not all: standing as I did on a quantity of moist straw my feet grew unhealthy and tender, and the master used to say:

"I don't know what is the matter with this horse; he goes very fumble-footed. I am sometimes afraid he will stumble."

"Yes, sir," said Alfred, "I have noticed the same myself, when I have exercised him."

Now the fact was that he hardly ever did exercise me. I often stood for days together without stretching my legs at all, and yet being fed as if I were at hard work. This made me restless and feverish. One day my feet were so tender that, trotting over some stones with my master on my back, I made two such serious stumbles that, he stopped at the farrier's, to see what was the matter with me. The man took up my feet and examined them and then he said:

"Your horse has got the 'thrush,' and badly, too; his feet are very tender. This sort of thing we find in foul stables, where the litter is never properly cleaned out. Send him here to-morrow. I will attend to his hoof, and I will direct your man how to apply the liniment which I will give him."

Thrush is a disease that affects a horse's hoof. Horses are one-toed animals—in fact, each hoof is basically one big toe surrounded by a hard outer layer, much like the human fingernail. Just as a fingernail needs to be trimmed and cleaned, horses' hoofs need to be trimmed and cleaned to avoid infections.

The farrier ordered all the litter to be taken out of my box each day, and the floor kept very clean. Then I was to have bran mashes and not so much corn, till my feet were well again. I soon regained my spirits; but

Mr. Barry was so disgusted at being deceived by his grooms that he determined to give up keeping a horse, and to hire when he wanted one. I was therefore kept till my feet were quite sound, and then sold again, to a London cab driver.

Chapter 9

A New Start as a Cab Horse

My new master's name was Jeremiah Barker, but as everyone called him Jerry, I shall do the same. Polly, his wife, was just as good a match as a man could have. She was a plump, trim, tidy little woman, with smooth, dark hair, dark eyes, and a merry little mouth. The boy, Harry, was nearly twelve years old, a tall, frank, good-tempered lad; and little Dorothy, Dolly as they called her, was her mother over again, at eight years old. They were all wonderfully fond of each other. I never knew such a happy, merry family before or since.

Jerry had a cab of his own, and two horses, which he drove and attended to himself. His other horse was a tall, white, rather large-boned animal called "Captain." He was old now, but when he was young he must have been splendid. He had still a proud way of holding his

head and arching his neck. In fact he was a high-bred, fine-mannered noble old horse, every inch of him.

Captain had been broken in and trained as an army horse; his first owner was an officer of cavalry.

The next morning when I was well groomed, Polly and Dolly came into the yard to see me and make friends. Harry had been helping his father since the early morning and had stated his opinion that I should turn out "a regular brick." Polly brought me a slice of apple, and Dolly, a piece of bread, and made as much of me as if I had been the "Black Beauty" of olden time. It was a great treat to be petted again and talked to in a gentle voice and I let them see as well as I could that I wished to be friendly. Polly thought I was very handsome and a great deal too good for a cab if it was not for the broken knees.

"Well, of course, there's no one to tell us whose fault that was," said Jerry, "and as long as I don't know I shall give him the benefit of the doubt, for a firmer, neater stepper I never rode. We'll call him Jack, after the old one, shall we Polly?"

"Oh do," she said, "for I like to keep a good name going."

There are strict rules in naming thoroughbred horses that vary according to the species and breed. Many people register the horse's official name, but then call the horse by something different at home, often referred to as the "stable name."

The first week of my life as a cab horse was very trying. I had never been to London, and the noise, the hurry, the crowds of horses, carts, and carriages that I had to make my way through made me feel anxious and harassed; but I soon found that I could perfectly trust my driver, and I got used to it. Jerry was as good a driver as I had ever known, and took as much thought for his horses as he did for himself. In a short time I and my master understood each other as well as horse and man can do. But the best thing we had here was our Sundays for rest; we worked so hard in the week that I do not think we could have kept up to it but for that day.

My new master was kind and good, so goodtempered and merry that very few people could pick a quarrel with him. He was very fond of making little songs, and singing them to himself.

Harry was as clever at stable-work as a much older boy, and always wanted to do what he could. Then Polly and Dolly used to come in the mornings to help with the

cab—to brush and beat the cushions, while Jerry was giving us a cleaning in the yard, and Harry was rubbing the harness. There used to be a great deal of laughing and fun.

Winter came early, with a great deal of cold and wet. There was

snow, or sleet, or rain almost every
day for weeks, changing only for
keen driving winds or
sharp frosts. The horses
all felt it very much. In
dry cold, a couple of

good thick rugs will keep the warmth in us; but in soaking rain they are soon no good. Some of the drivers had a waterproof cover to throw over, which was a fine thing; but some of the men were so poor that they could not protect either themselves or their horses, and many of them suffered much that winter. When the weather was very bad many of the men would go and sit in the tavern close by. Jerry never went. It was his opinion that spirits and beer made a man colder afterward. Polly always supplied him with something to eat when he could not get home, and sometimes he would see little Dolly peeping from the corner of the street to make sure if "father" was on the stand. If she saw him, she would run off at full speed and soon come back with something in a tin or basket. Some hot soup or pudding that Polly had ready. It was wonderful how such a little thing could get safely across the street, often thronged with horses and carriages; but she was a brave little maid, and felt it quite an honour to bring "father's first course" as he used to call it. She was a general favourite on the stand and there was not a man who would not have seen her safely across the street if Jerry had not been able to do it.

Chapter 10

ELECTION DAY

One day, while our cab and many others were waiting outside one of the parks, a shabby old cab drove up beside ours. The horse was an old worn-out chestnut, with bones that showed. I had been eating some hay, and the wind rolled a little lock of it that way, and the poor creature put out her thin neck and picked it up, then looked about for more. I was thinking I had seen that horse before, when she looked at me,

"Black Beauty, is that you?"

It was Ginger! But how changed! The beautifully arched neck was now straight, the joints were grown out of shape with hard work; the face full of suffering, and I could tell by the heaving of her sides, and her cough, how bad her breath was. I sidled up to her. It was a sad tale that she had to tell.

After a twelvemonths' run off at Earlshall, she was sold to a gentleman. For a little while she got on very well, but after a longer gallop than usual the old strain returned, and she was again sold. She changed hands several times.

"At last," she said, "I was bought by a man who keeps a number of cabs and horses, and lets them out. When they found out my weakness they said I must go into one of the low cabs, and just be used up; that is what they are doing, whipping and working with never one thought of what I suffer."

I said, "You used to stand up for yourself if you were ill-used."

"Ah!" she said, "I did once, but it's no use; men are strongest, there is nothing we can do, but just bear it. I wish I was dead. I wish . . . I wish I may drop down dead." I put my nose up to hers, but I could say nothing to comfort her.

A short time after this a cart with a dead horse in it passed our cabstand. It was a chestnut horse with a long, thin neck. I saw a white streak down the forehead. I believe it was Ginger; I hoped it was, for then her troubles would be over.

Election day meant no lack of work for Jerry and me. The streets were very full, and the cabs, with the candidates' colours on them, were dashing about through the crowd as if life and limb were of no consequence. The horses were having a bad time of it, poor things, but the voters inside thought nothing of that; many of them were half-drunk, hurrahing out of cab windows.

Jerry put on my nose-bag; "We must eat what we can on such days as these, so munch away, Jack."

I found I had a good feed of crushed oats wetted up with a little bran; this would be a treat any day, but very refreshing then. Jerry was so thoughtful and kind—what horse would not do his best for such a master?

I had not eaten many mouthfuls before a poor young woman, carrying a heavy child, came along. She seemed quite bewildered. Presently she asked if Jerry could tell her the way to St. Thomas's Hospital. She had come from the country that morning, she said she did not know about the election, and was quite a stranger in London. She had got an order for the hospital for her little boy. The child was crying with a feeble, pining cry.

"Poor little fellow!" she said. "He suffers a deal of pain; the doctor said if I could get him into the hospital he might get well; pray, sir, how far is it; and which way is it?"

"Why, missis," said Jerry, "you can't get there walking through crowds like this! Now look here, just get into this cab, and I'll drive you safe to the hospital. Don't you see the rain is coming on?"

"No, no, no, sir; I can't do that, thank you, I have only just enough money to get back with. Please tell me the way."

"Now look here, missis," said Jerry, "I've got dear children at home, I know a father's feelings; now get you into that cab, and I'll take you there for nothing."

"Heaven bless you!" said the woman, and burst into tears.

As Jerry went to open the door, two men with candidates' colours in their hats and buttonholes, ran up calling out, "Cab!"

"Engaged," cried Jerry; but one of the men, pushing past the woman, sprang into the cab, followed by the other. Jerry looked as stern as a policeman.

"This cab is already engaged, gentlemen, by that lady."

"Oh! She can wait;" said one of them, "Our business is very important, be-sides we were in first, it is our right, and we shall stay in." Jerry shut the door upon them.

"All right, gentlemen, pray stay in as long as it suits you; I can wait while you rest yourselves." And turning his back upon them he walked up to the young woman.

"They'll soon be gone," he said, laughing; "don't trouble yourself, my dear."

And they soon were gone, for when they understood Jerry's dodge they got out, calling him all sorts of bad names. After this we were soon on our way to the hospital. He watched her go in at the door. Then he patted my neck, which was always his way when anything pleased him. The rain was now coming down fast, and just as we were leaving, the hospital door opened again, and the porter called out, "Cab!" We stopped, and a lady came down the steps. Jerry seemed to know her at once. She put back her veil and said, "Barker! Jeremiah Barker, is that you? To the Paddington Station, and if we are in good time, you shall tell me all about Polly and the children."

We got to the station, and the lady stood a good while talking to Jerry. She had been Polly's mistress, and after many inquiries about her she said:

"How do you find the cab work suits you in winter? I know Polly was rather anxious about you last year."

"Yes, ma'am, she was. You see, ma'am, it is all hours and all weathers, and that does try a man's constitution; but I am getting on pretty well, and I should feel quite lost if I had not horses to look after."

"Well, Barker," she said, "it would be a great pity that you should seriously risk your health and if ever you think you ought to give up this cab work let me know."

Then, sending some kind messages to Polly she put something into his hand, saying, "There is five shillings each for the two children."

Jerry thanked her and seemed much pleased.

Chapter 11

NEW YEAR'S EVE

Christmas and the New Year are very merry times for some; but for cabmen and cabmen's horses it is no holiday, though it may be a harvest. There are so many parties and balls. Sometimes driver and horse have to wait for hours in the rain, shivering with the cold, while the merry people within are dancing away to the music. We had a great deal of late work in the Christmas week, and Jerry's cough was bad.

On the evening of the New Year we had to take two gentlemen to a house in one of the West End Squares. We set them down at nine o'clock, and were told to come again at eleven. "But," said one, "as it is a card

party, you may have to wait a few minutes, don't be late."

As the clock struck eleven we were at the door, for Jerry was always punctual. The wind had been very changeable, with squalls of rain during the day, but now it came on sharp, driving sleet, which seemed to come all the way round; it was very cold, and there was no shelter. At half-past twelve Jerry rang the bell and asked the servant if he would be wanted that night.

"Oh, yes, you'll be wanted," said the man; "you must not go, it will soon be over."

At a quarter-past one the two gentlemen got into the cab without a word. My legs were numb with cold, and I thought I should have stumbled. When the men got out they never said they were sorry to have kept us waiting so long, but were angry at the charge. At last we got home. Jerry could hardly speak, and his cough was dreadful.

"Can't I do something?" Polly said.

"Yes; get Jack something warm, and then boil me some gruel."

He could hardly get his breath, but he gave me a rub down as usual. Polly brought me a warm mash then they locked the door.

Late the next morning only Harry came. He cleaned and fed us, swept out the stalls, then put the straw back again as if it was Sunday. He was very still, and neither whistled nor sang. At noon he came again and gave us our food and water; this time Dolly came with him; she was crying, Jerry was dangerously ill. The doctor said that he must never go back to the cab work again if he wished to be an old man.

One afternoon Dolly came in, looking very full of something.

"Who lives at Fairstowe, Harry? Mother have got a letter from Fairstowe; she seemed so glad."

"Why, it is the name of Mrs. Fowler's place—mother's old mistress, the lady that father met last summer. I wonder what she says; run in and see, Dolly."

In a few minutes Dolly came dancing into the stable.

"Oh! Harry, Mrs. Fowler says we are all to go and live near her. There is a cottage that will just suit us, with a garden and apple-trees, and everything! Her coachman is going away in the spring, and then she will want father in his place. Mother is laughing and crying and father does look so happy!"

It was quickly settled that as soon as Jerry was well enough they should remove to the country, and that the cab and horses should be sold as soon as possible. This was heavy news for me, for I was not young now, and could not look for any improvement in my condition. Since I left Birtwick I had never been so happy as with my dear master Jerry; but three years of cab work will tell and I felt that I was not the horse that I had been.

The day came for going away. Jerry had not been allowed to go out yet, and I never saw him after that New Year's eve. Polly and the children came to bid me goodbye.

"Oh, poor old Jack, dear old Jack, I wish we could take you with us," she said, and then laying her hand on my mane, she put her face close to my neck and kissed me. Dolly was crying and kissed me too. Harry stroked me a great deal but said nothing, only he seemed very sad. And so I was led away to my new place.

I was sold to a corn dealer and baker, whom Jerry knew, and with him he thought I should have good food and fair work.

In the first he was quite right, but there was a foreman who was always hurrying and driving everyone, and frequently when I had quite a full load he would order something else to be taken on. My carter, whose name was Jakes, often said it was more than I ought to take, but the other always overruled him.

"'Twas no use going twice when once would do," and he chose to get business forward.

Good feed and fair rest will keep up one's strength, but no horse can stand against overloading; and I was getting so thoroughly pulled down from this cause that a younger horse was bought in my place and I was sold to a large cab owner.

Chapter 12

HARD TIMES WITH NICHOLAS SKINNER

My new master I shall never forget; he had black eyes, his mouth was as full of teeth as a bulldog's. His name was Nicholas Skinner.

Much as I had seen before, I never knew till now the utter misery of a cab-horse's life. Skinner was hard on the men, and the men were hard on the horses. We had no rest. Sometimes on a Sunday morning a party of fast men would hire the cab for the day. I had to take them ten or fifteen miles out into the country, and back again; never would any of them get down hill unless the driver was afraid I should not manage it, my driver was just as hard as his master. He had a cruel whip with something so sharp at the end that it sometimes drew blood, and he would even whip me under the belly, but still I did my best; for, as poor Ginger said, it was no use; men are the strongest.

My life was now so utterly wretched that I wished I might, like Ginger, drop down dead at my work. One day my wish very nearly came to pass.

We had to take a fare to the railway. A long train was just expected in, so my driver pulled up to take the chance of a return fare. We were called by a party of four; a noisy, blustering man with a lady, a little boy and a young girl, and a great deal of luggage. The young girl came and looked at me.

"Papa," she said, "I am sure this poor horse cannot take us and our luggage, he is so very weak and worn out."

"Oh! No, no, no, no, he's all right, miss," said my driver.

"Papa, papa, do take a second cab," said the young girl. "I am sure we are wrong, I am sure it is very cruel."

"Nonsense, Grace, get in the cab at once, don't make all this fuss; the man knows his own business. Get in and hold your tongue!"

Box after box was dragged on the top of the cab.

I got along fairly till we came to Ludgate Hill; but there the heavy load and my own exhaustion were too much. My feet slipped from under me, and I fell heavily on the ground on my side. I lay perfectly still; indeed I thought now I was going to die. I heard loud, angry voices, and that sweet, pitiful voice saying,

"Oh! That poor horse! It is all our fault."

Then I could hear a policeman giving orders, but I did not even open my eyes;

I could only draw a gasping breath now and then. Cold water was thrown over my head and something was covered over me. I cannot tell how long I lay there, but I found my life coming back, and a kind-voiced man was encouraging me to rise. I staggered to my feet, and was gently led to some stables which were close by. Here I was put

into a stall, and some warm gruel was brought, which I drank thankfully.

In the evening I was sufficiently recovered to be led back to Skinner's stables. In the morning, Skinner came with a farrier to look at me.

"This is a case of overwork more than disease," he said, "and there is not an ounce of strength left in him."

"Then he must just go to the dogs," said Skinner. "I work 'em as long as they'll go, and then sell 'em for what they'll fetch, at the knacker's or elsewhere."

A knackery is a type of slaughterhouse for work animals who have died or can no longer work. They are often processed into pet food or fertilizer.

"There is a sale of horses coming off in about ten days," said the farrier, "if you rest him and feed him up, you may get more than his skin is worth."

Upon this advice, Skinner unwillingly gave orders I should be well fed. Ten days of perfect rest, plenty of good oats, bran mashes, with boiled linseed mixed in them, did more to get up my condition than anything else could have done.

Chapter 13

A NEW BEGINNING

Then I was taken to the sale, a few miles out of London, so I held up my head, and hoped for the best.

At the sale I found myself in company with the old broken-down horses, some lame, some broken-winded, some old, and some that I am sure it would have been merciful to shoot. It was an anxious time!

Coming from the better part of the fair, I noticed a man, with a young boy by his side; he had a broad back and round shoulders, a kind, ruddy face. When he came up to me and my companions he gave a pitiful look round upon us. I saw his eye rest on me; I had still a good mane

and tail, which did something for my appearance. I pricked my ears. "There's a horse, Willie, that has known better days. He might have been anything when he was young; there's a deal of breeding about that horse." He gave me a kind pat on the neck. I put out my nose in answer to his kindness; the boy stroked my face.

"Poor old fellow! Could not you buy him and make him young again as you did with Ladybird?"

"My dear boy, I can't make all old horses young; besides, Ladybird was not so very old, as she was run down and badly used."

"Well, grandpapa, I don't believe that this one is old. Look into his mouth, and then you can tell. Ask the price; I am sure he would grow young in our meadows."

The man who had brought me for sale now put in his word.

"The young gentleman's a real knowing one, sir. This 'ere hoss is just pulled down with overwork in the cabs; he's not an old one, and I heard that a six months run off would set him right up, being as how his wind was not broken. 'Twould be worth a gentleman's while to give a five-pound note for him, and let him have a chance."

The little boy looked up eagerly. The farmer slowly felt my legs, then he looked at my mouth.

"Just trot him out, will you?"

I arched my poor thin neck, raised my tail a little, and threw out my legs as well as I could, for they were very stiff.

"What is the lowest you will take for him?" said the farmer as I came back.

"Five pounds, sir; that was the lowest price my master set."

Five pounds was still a fair amount of money back then.
It would be worth about one hundred dollars today.

"'Tis a speculation," said the old gentleman, shaking his head, but at the same time slowly drawing out his purse, "quite a speculation!"

"I can take him for you to the inn, if you please."

"Do so."

They walked forward, and I was led behind. The boy could hardly control his delight, and the old gentleman seemed to enjoy his pleasure. I had a good feed at the inn, and was then gently ridden home by a servant of my new master's, and turned into a large meadow with a shed in one corner of it.

Mr. Thoroughgood, for that was the name of my benefactor, gave orders that I should have hay and oats every night and morning, and the run of the meadow during the day, and, "Willie," said he, "I give him in charge to you."

I grew very fond of him. He called me Old Crony, as I used to come to him in the field and follow him about. Sometimes he brought his grandfather, who always looked closely at my legs.

"He is improving so steadily that I think we shall see a change for the better in the spring."

The perfect rest, the good food, the soft turf, the gentle exercise, soon began to tell on my condition and my spirits. My legs improved so much that I began to feel quite young again. One day in March Mr. Thoroughgood tried me in the phaeton and he and Willie drove me a few miles. I did the work with perfect ease.

"He's growing young, Willie; we must give him a little gentle work now, by mid-summer he will be as good as Ladybird."

"Oh, grandpapa, how glad I am you bought him!"

"Well, he has to thank you more than me; we must now be looking out for a quiet, genteel place for him, where he will be valued."

Chapter 14

MY LAST HOME

One day during this summer the groom cleaned and dressed me with such care that I thought some new change must be at hand. I think the harness had an extra polish. Willie seemed half-anxious, half-merry, as he got into the chaise with his grandfather.

"If the ladies take to him," said the old gentleman, "they'll be suited and he'll be suited."

A mile or two from the village we came to a pretty, low house, with a lawn and shrubbery at the front and a drive up to the door. Willie rang the bell, and asked if Miss Blomefield or Miss Ellen was at home. They were. Mr. Thoroughgood went into the house. In about ten minutes he returned, followed by three ladies; one tall, pale lady, wrapped in a white shawl, leaned on a younger lady, with dark eyes and a merry face; the other, a very stately-looking person, was Miss Blomefield.

The younger lady—Miss Ellen—took to me very much; I had such a good face. The tall, pale lady said that she should always be nervous in riding behind a horse that had once been down, as I might come down again, and if I did she should never get over the fright.

"You see, ladies," said Mr. Thoroughgood, "many first-rate horses have their knees broken through the carelessness of their drivers and from what I see of this horse I should say that is his case. If you incline you can have him on trial, and then your coachman will see what he thinks of him."

"You have always been such a good adviser to us about our horses," said the stately lady. "If my sister Lavinia sees no objection we will accept your offer of a trial, with thanks."

It was arranged that I should be sent for the next day. In the morning a smart-looking young man came for me. At first he looked pleased; but when he saw my knees he said in a disappointed voice:

"I didn't think, sir, you would have recommended my ladies a blemished horse."

"Handsome is as handsome does," said my master; "you are only taking him on trial. If he is not as safe as any horse you ever drove send him back."

I was led to my new home, and placed in a comfortable stable. The next day, when the groom was cleaning my face, he said:

"That is just like the star that 'Black Beauty' had. I wonder where he is now."

A little further on he came to the place in my neck where a little knot was in the skin. He almost started, and began to look me over carefully, talking to himself.

"White star in the forehead, one white foot on the off side, this little knot," then looking at the middle of

my back—"and, as I
am alive, there is that little patch of white hair.

It must be Black Beauty!
Why, Beauty! Beauty!
Do you know me?—Little
Joe Green, that almost
killed you?"

And he began patting and patting
me as if he was quite overjoyed. Now he was
a fine grown young man, with black
whiskers and a man's voice, and I was

very glad. I put my nose up to him, and tried to say that we were friends. I never saw a man so pleased.

"Give you a fair trial? I should think so indeed! I wonder who the rascal was that broke your knees, my old Beauty? You must have been badly served somewhere; well, well, it won't be my fault if you haven't good times of it now."

In the afternoon I was put into a low park chair and brought to

the door. Miss Ellen was going to try me, and Joe went with her. She seemed pleased with my paces. I heard Joe telling her about me, that he was sure I was Squire Gordon's old "Black Beauty."

When we returned, the other sisters came out to hear how I had behaved myself. She told them what she had just heard, and said:

"I shall certainly write to Mrs. Gordon, and tell her that her favourite horse has come to us. How pleased she will be!"

After this I was driven every day for a week or so, and as I appeared to be quite safe, Miss Lavinia at last ventured out in the small close carriage. After this it was decided to keep me and call me by my old name of "Black Beauty."

I have now lived in this happy place a whole year. Joe is the best and kindest of grooms. I feel my strength and spirits all coming back again. Mr. Thoroughgood said to Joe;

"In your place he will last till he is twenty years old—perhaps more."

My ladies have promised that I shall never be sold, and so I have nothing to fear; and here my story ends. My troubles are all over, and I am at home. Often before I am quite awake, I fancy I am still in the orchard at Birtwick, standing with my old friends under the apple-trees.

About the Author

Anna Sewell was born on March 30, 1820, in England. A childhood injury prevented her from walking well, so she spent much time riding in horse-drawn carriages. She originally wrote *Black Beauty* to encourage others to treat horses with kindness; little did she know the book would become a best-selling novel. *Black Beauty* was Sewell's only novel; however, she is remembered for her many efforts to improve the treatment of animals.

THE SECRET GARDEN

Frances Hodgson Burnett

Read by Jenny Agutter

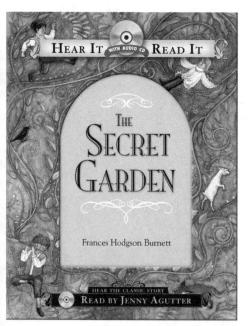

Mary Lennox doesn't want to move to England to live with her uncle, but she has no choice. At first she hates her uncle's cold house, the gardens, and moors that surround it, and the servants with their funny way of talking. And at night, she hears a child crying, but the servants insist it's only the wind. Curious in spite of herself, Mary wanders the house and gardens and discovers that both are full of secrets.

$9.99 U.S/$10.99 CAN/£6.99 UK   ISBN-13: 978-1-4022-1244-4
                                 ISBN-10: 1-4022-1244-5

KING ARTHUR
AND THE KNIGHTS OF THE ROUND TABLE

Benedict Flynn

Read by Sean Bean

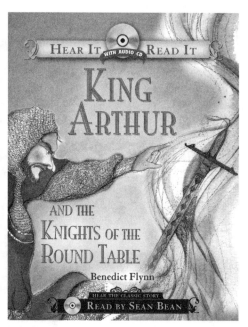

In *King Arthur and the Knights of the Round Table*, young Arthur is as surprised as anyone the day he pulls the mysterious sword from the stone and becomes the king of England! The wizard Merlin leads him to assemble his knights, including brave Sir Lancelot and pure Sir Galahad. Arthur and his knights undertake many quests to bring peace to the kingdom, and uphold justice for all. But all the while, the evil Morgana le Fay and Mordred plot to overthrow Arthur and rule themselves. Soon Arthur enters a terrible battle . . . for his kingdom, and his life.

$9.95 U.S/$11.95 CAN/£6.99 UK   ISBN-13: 978-1-4022-1243-7
ISBN-10: 1-4022-1243-7

THE ADVENTURES OF TOM SAWYER

Mark Twain

Read by Garrick Hagon

Tom Sawyer would rather not go to school. Instead, he and his friends Huck and Joe spend their time playing pirates, exploring caves and searching for buried treasure. When Tom and Huck witness a murder in a graveyard late one night, only they can save the town, their friends and the treasure from the evil Injun Joe. But are they brave enough to catch him? Maybe even mischievous boys can become heroes.

$9.95 U.S/$11.95 CAN/£6.99 UK   ISBN-13: 978-1-4022-1167-6
ISBN-10: 1-4022-1167-8